To children

of all ages

who celebrate

autumn with a visit

to the pumpkin patch

PUMPKIN HEADS!

Wendell Minor

SCHOLASTIC INC.

New York Toronto London Auckland Sydney Mexico City New Delhi Hong Kong Buenos Aires

October is here.
It's time to pick
a pumpkin!

On Halloween
every pumpkin
becomes
a pumpkin head.

Some are big.
Some are small.

Some may float
high in the sky.

Some peek
from
windows.

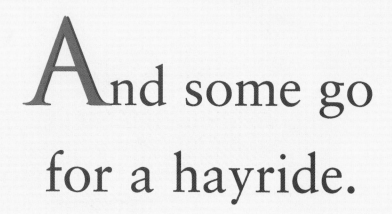

And some go
for a hayride.

Some pumpkin heads pretend to be cowboys...

or

snowmen...

or

witches!

Some
pumpkin heads
will greet
for trick-or-treat!

And

some will

scare crows.

Pumpkin heads
can be found
in the strangest
places.

But no matter where
you may find them,
pumpkin heads
of all shapes and sizes…

hope you have a

HAPPY HALLOWEEN!

This book was originally published in hardcover by the Blue Sky Press in 2000.

ISBN 0-439-46514-1

12 11 10 9 8 7 6 5 4 3 2 1   1 2 3 4 5 6/0

Printed in the U.S.A.   14

First Scholastic paperback printing, September 2001